A great book especially
*read with a vivid descri_*
*made. Very much recom_*
- hearted humour!

_____ Matovic

A really good read. I finished it in one sitting. I felt very close to the main character, Molly, and the people around her, the writing is clear and heartfelt.

A music therapist's work, a performer's self - doubt, an empath's challenges, all fascinating subjects in themselves, are woven together to take the reader on an interesting exploration of a young woman's quest for self - acceptance. Thoroughly recommended!

Ruth Fishman

A hugely enjoyable book that takes you on a journey of discovery from Camden Town to the coast of California, as one young woman goes in search of happiness. The characters are engaging and the settings are vividly described. Makes you want to go on a journey of discovery of your own.

Jenny Mill

Looking for Melody

Rachael Cook

Dear Julie,

Hope you enjoy my book!

love Rachael. xx

Published by New Generation Publishing in 2021

First Edition

ISBN   978-1-80369-031-5

www.newgeneration-publishing.com

New Generation Publishing

To the dream of returning to California someday…
……my heart cried out for you California
Oh California I'm coming home
Oh make me feel good rock 'n' roll band
I'm your biggest fan
California I'm coming home……

(Joni Mitchell)

Chapter 1: A Friday Night in Islington

"… Goodbye Jacob, Goodbye Molly, Goodbye, Goodbye, and see you very soon……"

The tiniest hand movement signified Jacob's Goodbye as the song drew to a close and Molly's heart soared at the possibility of progress. She had been working with Jacob for two months now, approximately four sessions, with not much response. Although the doctor had reported that the child was experiencing fine motor movements in both arms and legs, the recovery of his spirits did not seem to mirror his physical progress. Maybe the choice of music or music itself did not appeal to this child – how could one possibly know – that you weren't simply irritating or infuriating with your persistent chords and melodies? Molly knew that progress in the realm of music as therapy could be slow and that patience was an essential virtue. She was also new to her career and not as confident about her own approach as she would like to be.

She sighed inwardly, put her guitar to one side and made the obligatory small talk with Jacob's hopeful mother – who had been waiting outside in anticipation of a breakthrough – however tiny.

Then she swung into the office, collected her helmet and bag and wished a happy weekend to the receptionist on her way out of the door.

The sunshine and wind made a bracing combination as she headed down Chapel Market and rounded the corner to Marks and Spencer.

Emerging 15 minutes later with a ready meal and a bottle of Sauvignon Blanc, she felt ready for her Friday evening.

Speeding down Upper Street, she felt thrilled at that familiar feeling of freedom and relief to be moving with the wind in her hair in a city where nature sometimes seemed absent. Cycling was the only form of exercise that didn't feel, to her, like an endurance test. Rather it filled her with a sense of independent hope for all that awaited her. Exercising with such a sense of purpose (actually getting from A to B on a daily basis) warded off the dark thoughts that threatened to rear ugly heads if she didn't keep herself fit and healthy. As she rounded the home stretch of her journey and gracefully dismounted she thought once again how lucky she had been to find her rental studio flat – ex-council and in surprisingly good condition, on an estate verging the back streets of Islington. The huge benefit was a private roof garden, where she was cultivating sunflowers, cornflowers and all manner of other wildflowers and herby concoctions. Someone had given her a book on the healing power of herbs last Christmas and, fascinated, she had started her own little herb garden and begun brewing all sorts of teas and trying new recipes, experimenting with the effects.

Of course she paid over the odds for the luxury of a one bedroom flat with a garden, and only just broke even at the end of each month, but it was near to work and worth every penny for the maintenance of her peaceful state of mind and independence.

After securing her first job as a music therapist just over a year ago, she had seen a notice on the board at work. Someone was leaving London in search of a music therapy job in Australia, and wanted to rent out her flat privately, preferably to someone in the same profession. Molly jumped at the chance, and instantly warmed to her new landlady, Neave, a softly spoken Irish lady in her mid-thirties who came to be, in the short time Molly got to know her, something of a mentor and soulmate.

Molly often marvelled at the lucky breaks that seemed to have come her way recently. At the moment she seemed to attract positive opportunities and people – though it hadn't always been that way – and she wondered how long these golden opportunities would last.

Now Neave had found her dream job, working in her chosen profession in the beautiful setting of Byron Bay, New South Wales. In their frequent Skyping sessions, Neave spoke enticingly of the beauty of her location, hinting at how she would welcome visitors from the UK.

Half an hour later, as Molly was lapping up the last rays of sun with a sauvignon in one hand and the other resting on the rather worn arm of her grandpa's aging deckchair, Molly wistfully pondered a trip abroad as she sat back on the creaking chair, the noise mirroring her sense of relief to let go after a long day. She had inherited two of these chairs when he passed away last April, and though they were starting to rot in places they were a firm favourite for her roof garden afternoons.

Most of the time she managed to maintain a professional distance when dealing with clients who were physically or emotionally vulnerable, but occasionally emotions swept over her with an intensity that she found worrying and slightly frightening. She wasn't sure how to deal with these feelings in the context of her working environment, and had been meaning to broach the subject with Neave in the hope that she had experienced something similar in her first few years as a music therapist.

Her thoughts were interrupted by a faint buzz at her side, her mobile, still on silent after her session with Jakob, was alerting her to an early evening call from her mother. This was a 6pm tradition not to be broken lightly.

"Hello darling."

Joan Riding, 66 years old and in possession of a voracious appetite for whatever life had to offer, was a constant source of amazement to Molly, in that she had an insatiable capacity for giving and living, completing hundreds of tasks, it seemed, sometimes before Molly's own day had even begun.

"Hi mum, how are you? And how's dad?'

Barry Riding, on the other hand, was the anchor to steady Joan's generous social whirl. His calmness could sometimes be mistaken for apathy – but Molly knew better. Underneath the uncrumpled surface was a genuinely kind and thoughtful nature.

"Oh, you know, sitting around as unruffled as usual in his beloved garden!" And how was your day? How are you getting on with little Jakob?"

"Oh, I'm getting there slowly, little by little. How was your day? Any more news on the wedding?"

Molly's older sister Eva was getting married in May in a marquee in her parents back garden. It wouldn't have been Molly's choice of venue but there was great excitement all round with the oncoming preparations.

"Oh Eva's so laid back about it all! I thought wedding planning was supposed to be one of the most stressful things you will do in your lifetime but not for Eva. So no progress there!"

And then…..

"Just like dad"

"Just like dad"

And they both laughed. Saying the same thing, thinking the same thing, even feeling the same thing had been a trait common to the female line in her family since she could remember. It was both unnerving and comforting at the same time, an anomaly common amongst her family and friends.

At the end of the phone call she was left feeling both relieved and disappointed to be alone. With her thoughts and her solitary wine glass the evening stretched out in front of her. She thought about her family and the closeness that bound them. Eva and Molly had always got on like friends rather than sisters, plotting adventures and formulating plans. Happiness and heartbreak shared and felt intensely. In fact, they had planned, after they both finished university, (Eva two years earlier) to go travelling together for as long as it took for them to map out their individual futures and find something, anything that suited.

Then Eva had met Matt and he became the substitute travel companion, consigning Molly to a state of indecision. Not wanting to travel alone and torn between the choice of following her career or a trail across the world, she lingered in Islington until it all became clear, feeling constantly on the verge of change and upheaval.

What would it be like, she wondered, to leave it all behind and set off on her own to wherever she wished? Could she put her career on hold like that? Would she lose her grip on reality, or London reality as she knew it?

The ping of the microwave interrupted her thoughts as her stomach growled in anticipation. Time for a Friday night in, again….

Chapter 2: Let The Music Play

The butterflies in Molly's stomach were starting and it was time for a drink. Always the same for the couple of hours leading up to an open mic – the fear set in early.

Molly had always loved singing, but came from a household where music making had simply never occurred. The radio was often on and occasionally her parents sang along, and that was the extent of it. She only started considering herself 'musical' in any sense or form when she met Mrs. Lovett in the first year of secondary school. Mrs. Lovett was a music teacher who fiercely defended the importance of singing at all social occasions and in all formats, whenever possible in school life! She started choirs, championed music in school assemblies, rallied for funding to teach musical instruments and was the first person who ever encouraged a hope of talent in Molly. She nurtured the idea in her that music was important and that her singing had potential. She urged her to try solos and take up guitar, and really provided the push Molly needed all the way through secondary school to start upon that pathway to musical competence and to believe that a career in music was actually possible. When she applied to Bristol to do a music degree her parents did not object, but maintained a look of worry on their faces that spoke volumes about their fears for their daughter's future. Molly herself only half believed that she was good enough to stay on this musical journey, and this half belief was what still nagged at her now, as she stood on Parkway wondering why she put herself through this again and again.

The queue outside The Green Note seemed longer than usual, probably because it was a warm spring evening, no terrible hardship to be standing outside for an hour until the doors opened.

Molly loved this venue. It was small and intimate and usually filled with other musicians and their empathetic ears. Her best friend Josie was meeting her in the queue, but she could already see some regulars she recognised. After the usual chit chat to pass the time she saw a brightly dressed, slightly dishevelled but unwaveringly glamorous figure coming towards her up the gradual hill of Camden Parkway.

They exchanged excited greetings and headed inside as the doors edged open and everyone began to shuffle in. When they were seated and Molly had claimed her slot (eighth – not too near the beginning or end of the show) they found themselves with 20 or so minutes to catch up before the music began.

'So how's it going and how is the elusive new love interest coming along? ' Molly had been dying to know what had happened on Josie's second date with a promising new man she had met online.

'Oh, you know, still interested but not blown away with wild passion and desire! He's a good kisser and we're not short of banter and laughs but…….I don't know – what am I hoping for – too much do you think?'

'You know what they say about slow burn and instant ignition – maybe he's a slow burn man and will turn out to be the love of your life? Give him a chance!'

Josie was an idealist who was looking to be swept off her feet and away from it all. She lived in a world of glamour and aestheticism, an artist who struggled to get by with her occasional shows and random set of middle class students, and yet always hoped for the best of everything, living beyond her means more than was realistically sensible.

This was firm conversational fodder however, and kept the two chatting until the host took the mic and they joined the silence which fell all around them as everyone focused on the acts of the night.

Performing was something Molly felt compelled to do but which filled her with a nervousness that felt physical in the way it possessed her. As she approached the stage and sat gingerly down in the spotlight she tried to focus her mind and calm her trembling fingers as they brushed the strings of the guitar and struck up the first chords of her own composition, 'Roads Ahead'. As she breathed her lyrics into the microphone she felt herself begin to relax, and almost enjoy this exposure of her music. The audience responded with cheers of supportive approval and Molly went straight into her second song, an 'All About Eve' cover. She had discovered the band on a vinyl hunt one Saturday afternoon, browsing through the 80s section in a local record shop. 'And it takes more than the blues to bring me down….' Hopefully someone would recognise it and appreciate her version. She left the stage with wobbly legs and went straight to the bar, where a man in a cloth cap claimed that 'All About Eve' had been one of his favourite bands and it was lovely to hear it sung so well. Then the barmaid: 'Was that one of your own songs? I really loved the melody!' Satisfied with the acknowledgement of her efforts Molly returned to the table with her Rum and Coke, ready to relax and enjoy the rest of the show. She always made a point of approaching someone if she really enjoyed their songs – it was so important to get that acknowledgement and feel as if you had been noticed. Was it part of her own insecurity, that she needed this affirmation, or just human nature?

Molly preferred to stay right until the end to observe the etiquette of seeing all the acts. Having, on occasion, been on near the end when half the audience had left the building and only a handful of listeners remained, she felt this was the least she could do. She left with mixed feelings. Having been reassured by Josie that her set was 'lovely' and 'a good choice of songs' (she always did a cover and an original), she still felt unworthy. She felt that she was not exceptionally good, but that striving to be better was a treadmill that she felt she was pacing without view to an end. She sighed and gave Josie a fierce hug as they approached the tube station.

'Oww,' her friend said, 'sorry – it's just my shoulder – it seems to have been really sore recently, I can't move it comfortably at all, not sure what's going on.'

'Oh I'm sorry for irritating it, get it looked at, promise?'

Josie nodded and blew her a kiss as she headed for the Edgware branch of the Northern line.

One hour later (it seemed that everything in London took one hour nowadays) Molly closed the front door behind her and headed for her bed. She had never been one of these midnight snack and a late night film types, she simply put on some music and crashed out as soon as possible.

'Oww!' As she turned over in bed she felt a twinge in her shoulder. She turned to her other side and briefly remembered Josie's complaint. Strange coincidence…the thought was there and then it was gone as she drifted seamlessly into sleep.

Chapter 3: The Road to Recovery

It was Monday afternoon, and after a long morning of paperwork it was time to meet with Jacob once again. Molly had had a new idea, and as she set up the drum kit in anticipation she hoped she was onto a formula for success. Jacob's arm movements had improved a lot in the last few weeks, and so she got him seated at the kit with the help of his mum and showed him simple movements to help him make some noise. After the obligatory 'Hello' song, during which Jacob seemed generally unimpressed, she went over to the sound system to get things started.

She seated herself with her own hand held drum and waited for the beat to begin.

'Get yer rocks off get yer rocks off honey'…..chanted the music as Molly sang along and bashed her drum, hoping Jacob would attempt to mirror her actions. After a minute or two where Jacob sat with an expression of indecision – watching Molly with curiosity – she saw his head start to bob slightly. He looked at Molly's drum beating hand and then began to mirror her movements on the cymbal nearest to his right hand. Quietly at first, and then with as much vigour as he could muster, he banged along almost with the beat, and the corner of one side of his mouth lifted into a half smile. Molly laughed and gesticulated louder and harder, singing along as hard as she could. Jacob's half smile extended to a mini chuckle and Molly felt the joy soar in her own heart as they awkwardly mirrored each other in an on beat off beat fashion.

Despite sobering up somewhat during the wind down 'Goodbye' song, they seemed to have made some valuable progress. Molly was able to greet mum with a modicum of positive news and all three left the premises on a higher note than when they had entered.

Of course the ultimate goal was, alongside the speech therapist, to encourage Jacob to talk again. The car accident two months ago had left him with a debilitating brain injury, affecting his mobility and speech. Doctors could not guarantee his complete recovery, but everybody was hoping his condition was temporary. It was his low spirits that hit everybody concerned with his recovery the hardest, which was why today's small burst of enthusiasm had in turn affected Molly's own spirits so much. His mother, too, had left with a huge smile on her weary face, reflecting the hope that they were all that much closer to accessing a happier and healthier Jakob.

As Molly cycled home today her spirits were boosted further by the knowledge that tonight she was meeting Eva, not Eva and Matt, but Eva alone, for dinner. She would have her all to herself for once and relished the thought of returning to the girly familiarity of earlier times.

8pm and Molly arrived at the Thai on Camden High Street and seated herself near the window, flicking through the menu to get a head start on ordering so that the chatter may begin. She suddenly felt a bit nauseous and sipped on her water, switching to the drinks section to take her mind off food for a minute. Just a second later Eva emerged, tapping on the window with a beaming smile, characteristically 15 or so minutes late.

The two exchanged excited greetings and, as was customary, studied the menus simultaneously with a serious concentration so that they could get the ordering out of the way and fully enjoy each other's company.

'How about the Pinot Grigio – or a bottle of fizz?' suggested Molly eagerly.

'Err, not for me,' replied Eva, shifting uncomfortably in her seat.

'What!! What do you mean, not for me? You can't be serious?'

'Just don't feel like it.'

'No way – what are you not telling me?'

Eva glanced into the corner of the room and back again

'I'm not supposed to say…….'

'Oh my God you're not…….?'

Eva sighed, 'Two months tomorrow, but don't tell mum. I'm supposed to be keeping it quiet until up to three months'

'Shotgun wedding!' exclaimed Molly, 'Oh my GOD, I'm going to be an aunty!'

She jumped up, went round to Eva's side of the table and hugged her tightly.

'Well that's why I was late actually, I have been feeling very sickly and I had to tear myself away from the bathroom!' 'Probably need to eat'.

The feeling of nauseousness she had experienced flashed across Molly's consciousness for a milli second before the two lapsed into excited backward and forward analysis of the situation until the food arrived and silence descended for at least two minutes.

After the meal, with Eva feeling a little better and Molly sipping her third glass of Pinot (she had ordered the bottle anyway) the topic shifted to the women's everyday lives.

'Still no plans to travel then?' asked Eva tenuously, knowing this was a sore point and one which might open - up a whole barrel of hopes and fears.

'Oh, I don't know, I can't decide on where, when, who with, why even……and what's the point?'

'The point? The point? You can't possibly miss the point of travel? Err, opening your mind, expanding your life experience, adventure, excitement, etc, etc etc…'

'It's alright for you.' Growled Molly irritably, 'You had Matt to support you, I ….I'm scared you know, what if I hate it? Part of me is dying to get out of North London and see the world and part of me feels grounded to the idea of security and expectation.'

Eva sighed inwardly. It never ceased to amaze her how this talented, capable and independent woman sitting opposite her could doubt herself like this and display such an underwhelming lack of confidence. Wasn't she, Eva, the underachiever in this family, and yet wasn't she the one who felt most comfortable with her lot? Why couldn't Molly see the value in her own abilities and develop a confidence that would give her the courage of her convictions? 'Well, you'll never know what you are missing until you try it.' (A hopeful retort): 'Don't be left with regrets!' 'Do it!'

The conversation finally moved on to other things, but Molly was left with an unsettled feeling of resentment and jealousy. She was supposed to have been Eva's travel partner and now she was missing out…. stuck….. alone.

When she arrived home she found her head was spinning with ideas and riddled with indecision. She had a steady (if not that financially rewarding) job and a nice life. So what was missing and why did she feel so unsettled?   It wasn't that she wanted what Eva had, family and relationships were not what she was craving right now.   She was not remotely maternal. She was following what she had always imagined to be her vocation and yet she felt that some part of herself remained undiscovered.

First world problems - she thought to herself with a sigh as she turned off the light and drifted into a wine fuelled heavy snooze.

Chapter 4: Moving Onwards

After a conversation with Jakob's mum about his favourite music, Molly decided to try new tactics. Jakob was regaining a lot of movement in his arms and legs, so she intended to maximise on this while aiming, also, to work on the all - important speech process.

Singing was so often the key to re-finding one's lost speaking voice. Molly had spent a bit of time learning one of Jakob's favourite songs and was hoping he would join in on the chorus refrain. She had also fixed up a pedal drum which she was hoping he'd be able to use with the strength of two feet at once. She showed him the mechanism and he had a little try. She had fixed up her own too, so that he could mirror her actions.

She started off on guitar, hoping her own, sung version of the song would suffice, clunking down on the pedal with the beat and hoping Jakob would follow. After a fashion he made a movement with both feet, and then with the chorus: 'Girl you know I want your love….' A tenuous stamp, getting slowly stronger. But here was the piece de resistance – 'Oh I Oh I Oh I - Oh I' – hoping he would join in – she continued with the refrain, over and over, until, a little voice

… 'Oh a Oh a', followed by a clunk! Followed by another 'oh a', louder and louder until it was time to switch on the finale, the recorded version cued for that very moment, and off they went. Jakob sang and thumped, sang and thumped, until suddenly the pedal stuck, and he frowned and kicked, getting more and more frustrated, the anger apparent. As Molly watched she felt a wave of emotion, tears welling up, and felt sure that the root of that anger was a buried and insidious sadness. She jumped up and loosened the pedal mechanism, but the moment was gone, and Jakob looked downwards, squeezing weak little fists and waving his legs from side to side.

As Molly calmed him with a slow, soft version of the familiar goodbye song, extended and hopeful, she watched his little body slump and wondered at the torrent of emotion trapped deep inside that struggling child.

****

Later, as she sat at home, slumped in front of a blissfully innocuous TV programme, she thought about the morning's short journey from hope to despair and of the torrent of emotion that had grasped her. She almost felt like she had absorbed Jakob's frustration and mirrored back his emotions to him.

Browsing through Netflix looking for who knows what, something caught her eye. A documentary which seemed strangely appropriate to her thoughts and mood. Empaths – she had heard the word before – without really understanding what it meant, apart from trying to understand others' feelings. She watched the presented case study of a woman who unintentionally took on the mental states of those around her. Then another case of a man who physically felt the pain of others. Subsequently, they showed a centre in California which ran courses where people practiced these skills and learnt about managing their experiences and starting to heal themselves and others.

Fascinated, Molly wondered whether she herself had a tiny teeny smidgen of this 'condition?' and whether it was something she should explore further. When she had been in her early twenties she had suffered from depression and minor psychosis - a period in her life that was painful to think about now. Ashamedly, she remembered magnifying an ability to feel what others did in her mind. Her paranoid thoughts had created various scenarios around the fact that she had the power to feel what others felt. Obviously this paranoia was not something she wanted to dwell on now. Therefore, there were certain painful associations with thinking about the possibility that she may have some of the qualities of an empath. But was it worth exploring when she was feeling rational and happy? Could there be some truth in the phenomenon?

Now that she could examine her feelings in a more rational manner, she could see that sometimes her ability to empathise with others impacted strongly on her life. Realising that many people experienced this phenomenon, that it was potentially not just some warped psychotic fantasy, made her feel more curious and able to explore her feelings further. While feeling the physical symptoms of family and friends could be attributed to an instinctual connection quite basic in nature, it was questionable whether this type of human connection could be tapped into and used as a helpful therapeutic tool.

She had always wanted to go to California, and now the promise of a definite destination seemed even more appealing …

Chapter 5: Plans and Revelations

'Set in the heart of the Santa Cruz mountains, this peaceful paradise will restore your natural balance and calm and leave you feeling utterly rejuvenated, with a better understanding of your spiritual self.'

Santa Cruz had always been somewhere Molly had been interested in going, ever since her first encounter with the 1980s classic 'The Lost Boys', featuring the famous boardwalk and all that Californian charm.

She browsed through the drop down menus and feasted her eyes on the sumptuous gallery, featuring glorious sunsets over pristine sandy beaches, gleeful leaping dolphins and toasty wooden cabins set in Redwood backdrops.

Possible events for the month of June included, 'Mindful mountain walking,' 'Living with empathy and embracing self-love,' 'Women's meditation and yoga', 'Finding the self in the healing of others,' 'Renewal of minds and hearts,' 'Embracing the body' and so on and so on.

This could be a safe base from which to explore the best of California: The Big Sur, San Francisco, Yosemite, Hollywood and more. She could find out about herself and her 'abilities' while exploring one of the most beautiful and exciting parts of America.

After the wedding and encompassing a (long) summer holiday, maybe she could even keep her job and her flat, a travel compromise that suited all her needs and promised both adventure and some kind of personal growth.

Brought back down to earth with the familiar grating tone of her mobile (she had never got round to changing the generic tune), she switched her thoughts away from the screen. Eva calling. Probably wedding news.

'Hiya – what's up?' being chief bridesmaid, she was ready for some wedding preparation proposal or other.

'Dresses!' droned Eva in a less than excited tone.

'Mum says I've got to get onto it. We do need to wear something after all and I don't want her to end up having the final say!' 'Saturday? Spitalfields? 'Cherubs' and then 'Collectif' and we'll see what we can find? You up for it?'

'Fine. What time? Lunch first?'

'Probably not a good idea if we're trying on dresses. I think Mum was wanting to meet us later. How about a late lunch with her? The Real Greek?'

'Sounds good to me. I'll have a late breakfast.'

'Ok. 12.30 at the goat statue?'

'Yes, see you there! Bye!'

'See you then!'

'Cherubs' embraced the idea of colourful individuality while retaining an element of glamour and charm. Eva had made it very clear that she would not be wearing white and that no simpering frilliness would be tolerated. Since Molly was the only bridesmaid, they simply had to find two dresses that vaguely complimented each other while, obviously, the bridesmaid was not upstaging or over stating with her look.

'What colours were you thinking of? asked Molly, absentmindedly flicking through a rack of embroidered cardigans and circle skirts.

'Oh. Red? Blue? Green? But I'd really like red actually,'

It was true, red would set off Eva's olive complexion and dark bouncing curls perfectly.

'What about this?' Molly had found the most exquisite chiffon floaty dress in a deep scarlet with a layered skirt descending into long jagged points. The neckline was a delicate V and the waist pulled daringly inwards, which she knew Eva could get away with while she was still in the first trimester.

'Umm… I 'spose it's quite nice,' pondered Eva, sashaying the dress backwards and forwards from one hand to the other. Typical that Molly, with her excellent taste and eye for what suited her younger sister best, had spotted the dress first.

'Come on, try it on' coaxed Molly, 'and I'll try this.' She had found a red circle skirt with patent belt and a blouse, cream, adorned with little red cherries and bright red buttons.

The two emerged five minutes later complementing each other perfectly with their well-matched outfits.

'Well, what do you think?' asked a delighted Molly, thrilled that the dress suited her sister so well and complimented her figure and complexion.

Eva looked genuinely pleased, and after a few concerns on both sides had been ironed out they headed for the tills.

'Can't believe we bought the first thing we saw!!' says Molly with secret relief.

'No point in hanging around' retorted the no – nonsense Eva.

'Next stop accessories!'

'Not today though, that's enough for me. Let's go for a coffee before we meet mum!' and the two headed for Monmouth, satisfied with their successful morning purchases.

****

Half an hour later they arrived at the The Real Greek to find Joan already seated and looking with eager anticipation at their shopping bags.

After the excitement of 'show and tell' and a few approving murmurs they tucked into a mezze lunch and their usual catch up chat, tumbling over each other's words and making customary interruptions here and there.

When Molly mentioned that she was thinking of a summer trip Eva squealed with excitement and her mother nodded with more tempered enthusiasm. Waiting for the inevitable, ever practical questions about work and holiday allowance, rent and savings, she attempted to change the topic and test the waters with their opinions on the main focus for her trip.

'A retreat centre?' asked her mum quizzically. She could never understand why her intelligent, successful daughter (she had, financial prosperity aside, at last forged some kind of semi-stable career in music) needed to constantly pursue self-improvement. Why couldn't she just be happy in the moment, like Eva?

Meanwhile Molly tried to explain her plans, as plainly as possible, until it all gushed out in torrents of questioning words and phrases, her revelation about empaths and her research and ideas. How she had wondered if it was all at all applicable to her and what she could do to find out more about it.

While she was talking, Eva focused on her eagerly, all interest and enthusiasm, practically jumping out of her seat with excitement. She had loved her travel experience, and would happily do it all over again in the flash of an eye. The idea of a journey of self- discovery definitely appealed to her hippy side, but had the potential, she felt, to be overly investigative. Typical of Molly, with her seriously inadequate sense of self.

On the other side of the table, Joan tilted her head to one side as if deep in thought, waited for Molly to finish, and then contributed:

'When you were little, I thought you would make up stories to get out of school, walks and all manner of things you didn't want to do. One evening, the night before we were all due to drive to your Uncle Bob's for a family get together, you came down from your bedroom complaining of a sore tummy. Where does it hurt? I asked, and you pointed to your lower right side. I managed to get you settled with Calpol and hugs, and you finally went to sleep. That was the night before Eva got rushed to hospital with appendicitis. Makes me think now that maybe your gripes and moans meant something. I had never heard of an empath and it was always as quickly forgotten as it came on. Your pains very rarely developed into anything substantial.'

The three wiled away the afternoon with anecdotes, wondering about the truth of the matter. Eva seemed more convinced than Joan, forever the sceptic, but as Molly reminded them, all she was doing was research – not claiming powers that she did not understand or even perhaps approve of.

Later that evening Molly browsed the internet. The conversation had roused her interest and she was eager to find out as much as possible about the concept of empaths.

*Judith Orloff MD is the NY Times bestselling author of **The Empath's Survival Guide: Life Strategies for Sensitive People**, **Thriving as an Empath**, and **Emotional Freedom**.

Dr. Orloff is a psychiatrist, an empath and intuitive healer, and is on the UCLA Psychiatric Clinical Faculty. She synthesizes the pearls of traditional medicine with cutting edge knowledge of intuition, energy, and spirituality.

She found and scoured the website, coming across the following quote taken from Dr. Orloff's writing:

*Discovering that you are a physical empath can be a revelation. Rest assured: You are not crazy. You are not a malingerer or hypochondriac. You are not imagining things. You are a sensitive person with a gift that you must develop and successfully manage.

To what degree Molly possessed this 'gift' she was not sure. Was it worth exploring? Or was she opening a can of worms that would wriggle her ragged?

(* see Bibliography for reference)

Chapter 6: Loose Ends and New Ideas

For two weeks now Molly and Jakob had been working on a song to try and express some of his new, happier feelings. Using lines from other songs and incorporating a variety of percussion and other instruments, they had just about put together the final version and were having a run through before next week's recording session.

Jakob began with his one keyboard note in repetition and Molly joined him on guitar. Jakob's speaking had come along in leaps and bounds, and he had been able to choose the words and phrases he wanted to piece together with a selection of popular melodies.

'I can throw my hands up in the air sometimes
Singing ah oh, I can let go,
And I go on and on and on,
Singing my happy song, yeah,
Oh I oh I oh I oh I,
Oh I oh I oh I oh I
Oh I oh I oh I oh I
I can really love myself….'

Tao Cruz, Ed Sheeran and Justin Bieber would've been proud! There was a climax in the middle where the accompaniment stopped and Molly slammed down on the pedal drum while Jakob shouted out the words, and then a musical outro with Jakob banging on the claves.

Seeing Jakob leave with a genuine smile on his face had released that clenching feeling in Molly's heart and caused her to relax as if someone had squeezed an enormous sigh of relief out of her body, and was still squeezing. Jakob's mum seemed to have experienced a similar squeeze of relief, and was full of chatter about how she was having conversations with her newly invigorated little boy, who was, apparently, bursting into song at various and delightful moments throughout the day. The transformation was amazing. A combination of time, speech and music therapy, physio, patience and oodles of parental love had worked their slow but steady magic.

Molly didn't really want to take on more cases until after the wedding and the impending trip, which was starting to become a reality in the making. First of all she had to ensure she could take the holiday, and that was her job for this morning, to tackle her manager and secure a six-week break.

She emerged from the office half an hour later feeling as if someone was squeezing that last little bit of relief slowly out of her body and that the path to relaxation and a little bit of freedom lay stretching out in front of her. Summer was always a little slower at the clinic, and securing a 6 week June into July break had been no problem at all. Now she could really get started on the planning!

****

The 1st May and Eva's wedding day was finally upon them. Determined not to jinx the weather, Eva had only ordered one small marquee, and as usual her luck had held out and it was the most beautiful of sunny days with a slight, cooling breeze to complete the package of perfectness. Joan was fretting and buzzing round the house and garden while Barry carried chairs, ushered deliveries to their correct spots in the immaculately laid out and decorated garden and generally calmed all their nerves and soothed all their spirits.

Even Eva had a touch of the jitters, despite a Bucks Fizz breakfast which had extended into elevenses.

The paving stones which led to the field behind the Jenkins' garden and which guests were now beginning to make their way down, had been lined with tiny fairy lights and adorned with flowered trellises. The chairs were laid out in rows beside the twisting riverside and beneath the sweeping willow stood an arch adorned with corn and sun flowers where Eva and Matt would make their vows.

After a hitch-free ceremony consisting of self-penned vows, friends' poetry recitals and Molly's own rendition of Nat King Cole's 'L-O-V-E' they all made their way into the marquee in the garden for a reception consisting of a delicious buffet, a mere three tear- jerking speeches and an invitation for people to make their way onto the patio for more drinks and live music, followed by dancing if you so wished.

Molly found herself still seated at the head table with her dad and a half finished glass of sparkling champagne. Weddings tired her out and she needed to get her second wind. Sensing her weariness, Barry put his arm around Molly's shoulders and gave her a warm tight squeeze which brought tears to her eyes and calm to her heart simultaneously.

'I heard about your plan', started Barry carefully

'And what do you think dad?'

'Well, to be honest I wish I'd travelled more myself and I say go forth and explore yourself!'

'Explore myself?

'Well, you know what I mean, sow your seeds, throw your oats, live your life and have no regrets – all that.'

'Thanks Dad, glad I've got your approval!'

'Now, I must go and manage your mother's champagne intake before she grabs the microphone and makes for another speech.'

Barry was, Molly thought to herself, the glue holding together the most important women in his life. Behind the calm stood an instinctive knowledge of how to deal with their needs as calmly and intuitively as possible. An unsuspecting empath himself, surely.

Molly wandered out to the garden. Now the light was dimming and the fairy lights were coming into their own and filling the whole place with twinkle and glow.

There was a gypsy jazz band playing and she sat on the edge of the garden wall and soaked in the early evening atmosphere. She watched her sister as she maintained her normal degree of social whirl, dancing around her friends and relatives, refilling their glasses with fizz and their ears with her incessant excited chat.

'Oops, sorry!'

Molly felt a splash of something cold and sticky on her leg and turned to see a tall, blond and very tanned lady catch her falling wine glass by the stem just before it hit the hard stone of the patio paving. Eva had absolutely refused plastic glasses and so far her gamble had paid off, but it was early hours yet.

'That's ok' said Molly, brushing her leg absent-mindedly.

'Are you Eva's sister?'

Molly answered in the affirmative.

'Thought so, I'd recognise those cheek bones anywhere, a family trait?'

Molly glanced across at her dad's chubby rounded cheeks and smiled apologetically.

Once they had established that, yes, Molly was the younger one, and yes, she was the music therapist one and even that yes, she was heading off to America in a couple of months (what else had Eva been telling all her friends??) they managed to turn the tables on the conversation. A question that Molly hated:

'So, what do you do?' (quickly negated by) 'How do you know Eva?'

'Oh,I work in an alternative therapy centre. I got to know Eva from there. She comes in sometimes for a massage and I met her on reception.'

'Oh. What do you specialize in?'

'Reiki'

Molly had always been a bit sceptical about this. Holding hands over someone and expecting them to be healed. But what was she thinking, how did that equate with thinking she was an empath. Weren't the two equally unbelievable and unlikely? She took a deep breath and...

'I'm looking into healing and alternative therapies myself actually,' she ventured, 'but…'

'…but you're not sure if it works?' asked the smiling blond lady (she had not even asked her name!)

'Do you have to know?' she asked gently

'Do you actually understand how your mobile phone works or how you get a TV signal? It's all about the transmitting of energy. If we are ill or low in spirits we are low in energy and sometimes it just needs replenishing. Transferring from one source to another. Not all healing is faith healing. Even the sceptical can be healed… Ooh – I think that's my daughter calling for me – looks like she just fell off the trampoline! Oh dear, I'm sorry, maybe we can finish this conversation another time?'

And off she went, leaving a thoughtful Molly to re-evaluate her view of those things that, as yet, she was not sure of and didn't fully understand her attitude towards.

'Molly, Molly!' her dad's face was thrust suddenly into vision, an urgent look on his face,

'Come and help me decorate the car! They're off soon'

And so for the next 20 minutes Molly and Barry swathed the taxi and its bumper with tin cans, silver balloons, streamers and all sorts of other tat.

'D'you think it'll do?' asked Molly, requiring, it seemed, some acknowledgement of her abilities, the car symbolic somehow of what she could and would achieve.

'It'll take them far, just as your many talents, my love, will take you to exactly the place you want to be, you mark my words.'

And with that, they both watched the frenzied departure of the newly-weds. Molly filled with a warm realization that yet again her father had said exactly the right thing at the right time.

As Eva and Matt zoomed off into the night accompanied by dozens of tipsy hoots, and waves Molly sighed with boozy satisfaction and made her way back into her childhood garden, to be serenaded in her mind's eye by hazy dreams of the unknown journey which lay ahead of her.

Chapter 7: First Impressions

Sitting on the Highway 17 express from San Jose to Santa Cruz, Molly reflected on the last couple of weeks and wondered excitedly about what lay ahead of her.

Jakob's last session had acted as a satisfying closure for their time together. The recording had gone very well and had meant that they had produced a record of what Jakob had achieved over his 12 weeks of music therapy. His mum had been over the moon, and the two had presented her with a thank you book made up of pictures of Jacob's progress, the last page being one of Jacob's own drawings. It was his interpretation of her playing guitar and singing hello and goodbye. He had written a little thank you note underneath in only slightly spidery handwriting, showing how far he had come since the accident and his unhappy days.

Joan, Barry, Eva and Matt had all come to the airport to wave goodbye and see Molly safely on her way. Eva had found it hard to hide her excitement, bouncing eagerly from one foot to the other, her incessant talk littered with advice and forecasts. Joan, on the other hand, with Barry stoically squeezing her hand in support, blinked away the tears, and pressed a small package into Molly's hand, instructing her to open it only once she was in the air and finally on her way.

The brightly bound package had revealed a silver pendant in the shape of a carefully crafted compass, pointing West and opening into a locket. Inside which was a picture of the whole family, taken at the wedding.

Clutching it to her chest, she gazed out over the summit of whatever hill they had just surmounted at her first view of the glistening Monterey Bay. As they approached downtown Santa Cruz, Molly hoped the Redwood Heights Healing Centre would be everything she had expected. Though she had her apprehensions about living for 4 weeks in this alternative community, she was overwhelmingly hopeful about what she would learn there. She was enrolled on a course called 'Discovering The Healing Self', run by an experienced healing therapist: Barbara Hiffness (who had done extensive research into the healing role of empaths). She had been scouring the Redwoods brochure and planning her daily activities for the last month or so. She had decided she would start each morning with a Vinyasa Flow 'Rise and Shine' class, explore the discipline of Myofascial Release with an afternoon workshop, attempt a few Reiki sessions and of course make the most of the spa centre, where she would rekindle her swimming skills, as well as lounging in the Jacuzzi and steam/sauna whenever possible. This trip had only been possible due to an inheritance she had come into a couple of years ago when her Grandma Jill had passed away at the grand old age of 96, leaving her a tidy sum to store away for some future opportunity of her choosing. And here was the opportunity!

Pulling into the Santa Cruz downtown metro centre, Molly knew exactly where she was headed before catching the bus up to Redwood Heights. She wanted her first glimpse of the iconic boardwalk. Having kept her packing to a surprisingly reasonable limit, she was able to take her bag with her and head off down Front Street to get her first glimpse of the much coveted 'Lost Boys' backdrop!

Two hours later and Molly found herself outside Redwood Heights poised to push open the door to reception and discover her home to be for the next two weeks. Wind chimes swung lazily from porch timbers, overhanging cushion-strewn seats, surrounded by all sorts of greenery potted in brightly coloured urns of all shapes and sizes. It looked welcoming and suitably Zen, cocooned in its mountain side location, surrounded by sea views of Monterey Bay and promising Redwood walks around the site.

'Hi'. The door opened and Molly was greeted with a relaxed smile and a firm handshake.

'Are you here for one of the courses?'

'Yes. I'm Molly. Do you work here?'

'Yes, I'm Anya, the receptionist and co-host. Come in and I'll get you checked in and settled'

20 minutes later, after a tangy and refreshing homemade lemongrass punch and a tour of the main building, Molly found herself in a self-contained wood-side cabin with an en suite open air shower and private balcony complete with swinging wicker chair and partial sea view. She sighed with satisfaction and settled herself in the outside chair to go over the Redwood Heights daily schedule.

7.30am – morning: 'Rise and Shine' Vinyasa flow yoga

8.30am – 10am: Breakfast in the Redwoods Conservatory

11am: Session 1 of your chosen course of study:
'Discovering the Healing Self'
'The Healing Power of Crystals'
'Yogic meditation'
1pm: Lunch in Redwoods Conservatory
3pm: Treatment or workshop of your choice:
Flotation
Discovering Myofascial Release
Acupressure
Reiki for rejuvenation
Meditation and Mindfulness
6pm: Dinner in the Redwoods Conservatory

(All the food was vegetarian with vegan and gluten free options. Molly was vegetarian and had been toying with the idea of trying a vegan diet for a while now. Maybe now was the time to experiment)

8.30pm: 'Stretch and Bend' a relaxing evening yoga and meditation practice

This really did seem too good to be true. Molly looked at her watch, 5.30pm, half an hour until dinner. Just enough time to get herself unpacked, showered and sorted after her sticky journey across the Pacific Coast. The temperature was higher than she'd imagined and although it was slightly cooler on the mountainside, Molly was definitely in need of a refreshing shower.

****

The conservatory was as relaxed and bohemian in nature as the rest of the resort had so far appeared. Hues of blue, green and yellow adorned the chairs and tables, themselves nestled amongst an array of lush- looking hanging and standing plants. Windows and doors formed a complete glass surrounding looking out over the mountainside and the county beyond. Molly seated herself at a table for four (no smaller seating formations seemed available) and watched as the guests started to appear and arrange themselves accordingly. She felt slightly nervous about the idea of communal meal times and the uncomfortable polite conversation that that would inevitably entail.

'Hi. Mind if I join you?' Dressed in sweeping floor length clothes and swathed in friendship bands and strings of necklaces, the approaching woman seemed to perfectly compliment her bohemian surroundings, making Molly feel a bit of an outcast in her cut - off jeans, crocs and plain black t-shirt.

'Course not', she replied, ever the polite and accommodating Brit.

'I just got here and don't know the where's and whys just yet. What about you?' the soft Californian drawl rose in intonation at the end of each phrase in a way that was inviting and slightly unsettling at the same time.

'Me too,' smiled Molly. 'I just arrived from England this morning for a course starting tomorrow. I'm Molly by the way'. She held out her hand and was reassured by the firm grip which greeted her.

'Carola. Mine starts tomorrow too. 'The Healing Power of Crystals'. What about you?'

Molly noticed the large rose quartz shining from the woman's neckline.

'Discovering the Healing Self', answered Molly self-consciously. She still felt slightly ill at ease with the new path of self-exploration she had chosen.

Before the two could get better acquainted, a third reticent infiltrator approached their table. Tall and dark haired with a lean, well-sculptured physique, Molly's heart lurched somewhat as the tanned and smiling male newcomer stretched out his hand in welcome. 'Tom' he piped out cheerfully 'Pleased to meet you'.

As the conversation developed, around frequent trips to the lavishly overloaded buffet table, filled with reams of sumptuous vegetarian and vegan dishes, the identity of her fellow students slowly unravelled itself.

Tom had been living in San Jose for the past two years. Originally from Preston, he was currently working as a systems analyst for a large international company, a job which he furiously insisted was merely 'bringing in the bacon' and not a lifetime's dream vocation. In possession of a dry northern humour peppered with cheekiness, he was immediately appealing with his light-hearted approach to the situation in which they found themselves.

Carola's seriousness of attitude towards everything alternative and therapy - related created such a sharp contrast to Tom's that the opportunity for mismatched comedy moments was inherent. She worked in a 'spiritual' shop called 'Revelations' in the heart of San Francisco.

She spent her days ensconced in everything you may need to enhance your spiritual life – whiffs of incense, ceramic bowls filled with Angel cards, ripe for the picking, aromatherapy oils galore, shelves brimming with self - help manuals, and most importantly for Carola, a plethora of crystals of all origins. She spoke excitedly about discovering more about the healing power of these wondrous rocks and, refreshingly, lacked any trace of the cynicism which possessed Molly and was preventing, as yet, her whole-hearted immersion into the Redwoods experience.

'Uffhhggherm'. A tall, lean and bonily athletic looking man with salt and pepper stubble and fisherman's pants stood to make an announcement.

'Don't forget Stretch and Bend at the slightly earlier time of 8pm tonight. Sally usually takes this class, but I'll be standing in for her tonight. See you there.'

'Going?' asked Tom, raising one eyebrow testily

'I think so,' Molly replied. 'I need a stretch after today's journey. What about you Carola?'

'Oh no. Not me. I want to get an early night so I'm ready for my course tomorrow. Have fun though guys!'

Half an hour later and a handful of 'inmates' lay stretched on their backs in a pleasant dome-shaped hall waiting for their pathway to relaxation. Tom had placed his mat adjacent to Molly's, and she shifted restlessly, uncomfortably aware of his closeness in proximity.

'Right' started Ged, 'Lets get going. Most importantly, don't forget to breathe.'

'Hardly likely', murmured Tom from his prone position next to Molly

Ged's voice was not relaxing and impatience emanated from his person. Maybe not the right choice for a pre-bedtime relaxation session, thought Molly as she dutifully followed his instructions.

'Send your sitting bones earthbound' came the instruction and…

'Does that mean plonk your bum on the floor?' from the mat next door

Molly supressed a smile and continued with her bends and stretches alongside Ged's gruffly barked orders and Tom's whispered heckles. She was going to have to find a way to stop herself from sidling on towards the cynicism which was starting to beckon her forwards.

Chapter 8: Introductions

After a satisfyingly sound night's sleep, Molly's morning start was as relaxing and refreshing as last night had been tension - inducing and tiring. Sally's Vinyasa yoga had literally 'flowed' with calm and now she found herself sitting in yet another soothing plant-lined space awaiting the start of her course. Tom had arrived, plus another five or so students, all sitting patiently round in an expectant circle awaiting their tutor, Barbara Hiffness.

The door swung aside and a smartly dressed and well-presented lady in her mid to late 40s entered the room and smiled invitingly over towards the circle.

'Lovely to see you all here on time' she crooned in smooth, low tones. 'I'm Barbara and lets get started!'

Since she had arrived, having become accustomed to bohemian, crystal clad garb with a plethora of Thai fisherman's pants thrown in, Molly felt pleasantly surprised and relieved. As Barbara, sporting a crisp white shirt and smart pleated trousers, started to introduce herself Molly's relief widened into an authentic and accepting interest and she began to relax. Somehow, she noted to herself, looking more like a London City banker then Californian Faith Healer made Molly more able to take Barbara seriously!

'Empathy and communication are key to what we will learn and practice here.' Barbara began.

'We will have various ideas about the extent to which we believe in and want to embrace aspects of healing. I only ask that you approach others with acceptance and do try to suspend distrust or cynicism when faced with things you have not experienced or with which you are not familiar.'

'I would like to start by going round the circle and introducing ourselves and our reason for embarking on this course of study.'

Starting with herself, Barbara explained how she had come to healing late in life from a background of scientific research. She had her own theories about energy and connection which she would share as the sessions progressed. She had spent years grappling with the contradictions between spirituality and hard scientific fact.

Next to speak was Jenny, from North Carolina, who seemed eager to spill out her dilemma and unload her worries, sitting back in her chair smiling, with something like relief, when she had finished her introduction. It appeared she had been diagnosed with something called 'Mirror Touch Synesthesia', (a condition which causes a person to feel touch when they observe others being touched). Being a nurse, by vocation, this had considerable repercussions on her job. Nursing was, however, an occupation which she loved and was reluctant to give up on.

Neave, a self-employed reflexologist from Canada, had been overwhelmed with good reports from her clients and consequently wondered if she could take the healing process to another level by adopting different methods or approaches.

Next to speak was Celia, who ran her own alternative therapy clinic in central Los Angeles and was keen to find out more about healing with the view to putting on a wider range of courses in order to expand her client base.

Since she was something akin to an alternative practitioner herself, Molly saw fit to input at this point, explaining how her work involved connecting on a deeply empathetic level, and how she felt drawn to discovering more about her own susceptibility to empathy and healing. She told the group how she sometimes found herself becoming overly involved in others' feelings, unable to disengage and unsure where her own emotions ended and others began.

Finally, the two men, John and Tim, contributed their own personal stories to the group, starting with John, a parish priest from

San Francisco. John spoke, similarly, about how he felt others' emotions and pain deeply and often found it difficult to isolate and recognise his own feelings. Some parishioners relied heavily on him for support, which in turn left him drained and unable to cope with his own needs and desires. He was feeling so overwhelmed that ideas of leaving his job and seeking alternative employment had started to surface.

Tom's story, on the other hand, centred more around the pain and problems of his closest family and friends. He was a twin who had spent a lifetime bound closely to his brother, feeling his pain, taking on his emotions and even dreaming his dreams. This extended, however, to others who infiltrated his close circle of family and friends. Like Molly, Tom had kept quiet about these close to home experiences but now found himself wondering about their usefulness.

After listening to this heartfelt expression of highly believable concerns and experiences, Molly found herself beginning finally to engage seriously in the journey which lay ahead of her. Breathing a sigh of relieved anticipation, she followed the others into the conservatory for tea with a real sense that she was about to find out more about herself and her new found colleagues.

Chapter 9: Contemplation and Cocktails

'I will divide this course into four parts….'

On Day 2 of the course Barbara began to give an outline of where they were heading with all this:

Week 1:

Managing and sharing experiences
Introduction to healing. Is it for you?

Weeks 2 and 3:

Aspects of healing and practice – (this will be the longest section of the course with the sharpest learning curve)

Week 4:

What have you learnt and how do you see yourself progressing?

'Altruism. It's a word I don't like, but which some link closely to the concept of Empathy. I think everyone here has demonstrated that they possess or are at least familiar with aspects of being an empath. Feeling what others feel sometimes physically or sometimes emotionally. However, being an empath isn't just about selflessness. Using a gift that you have been given genetically or otherwise can be rewarding and somewhat vocational in its nature. The question is though, how do we balance the ability to relate to others so intensely with our everyday lives? We will explore this all week and hopefully by the end of the course feel better placed to use our empathetic tendencies in a more practical and productive manner. First, however, I would like us to share some experiences, so that we feel more able to understand the various strands of empathetic ability.'

Molly was paired with John, and each pair was asked to recall a time when they had experienced fear or discomfort at not being able to manage an empathetic experience. After their allotted thinking time, the two stared at each other in uncomfortable silence. Clearing her throat Molly ventured what she hoped was a reassuring smile and asked who should start. Very nervously, and to Molly's relief, John began his stilted tale, briefly hurtling onwards in a confusing mish-mash of words until gradually he began to relax, and Molly became totally absorbed in his story, fascinated by the tiny likenesses binding John's experience to her own.

He explained to her how being a parish priest could be compared, at times, to being a social worker, counsellor, or simply the best of friends. Last year, he began, a young woman had started visiting the vicarage with her young daughter, desperate for somewhere to turn. He had listened as she told him that she was a heroin addict and had nowhere left to go. Sent away by her parents and currently living with a violent drug-addicted partner she feared for her child and worried about providing basic needs for the girl. She was obviously depressed, and as John described the feeling of desolation and despair that had overcome him during those months, especially in the woman's presence, Molly held her breath. She remembered back to a time when Jakob's anger and fear had surged inside her until she had felt a need to disconnect.

Eventually, John went on, after attempts at getting social services involved, gifts of food and emergency cash and as much neutral advice as he could muster, the woman stopped coming. One evening a few weeks later John had felt overcome by a crippling anxiety followed by sharp pains in his abdomen and an exhausting tiredness that caused him to sleep for a solid 10 hours. Awaking in a similar state of anxious exhaustion, John had received a phone call informing him that the woman had been stabbed the previous evening by her angry partner and the girl had been immediately removed and taken in by local foster carers.

What if I had managed the situation better? John had asked himself. What if I had been able to heal her of her addiction and give her the right advice? And why was I not able to manage my own emotions and stand away from the woman's own despair, looking on, concerned but separate, as I managed the situation efficiently?

As Molly related her own stories of clients with whom her emotions had become so overly entangled that she had felt unable to identify with her own actual state of mind, she began to feel that she was not alone. She could see, however, that John seemed to experience an intensity in sharing physical and emotional pain with others that she could not begin to imagine. Her empathetic mirroring of Jakob's emotions, for example, did not impact on her ability to maintain her professional composure. John's was another level of experience which both fascinated and slightly scared her.

She could see that, in sharing their stories, the group were becoming better able to paint clearer pictures of their own behaviours.

After talking at length about the similarities in their own experiences and in their own abilities to manage the situations in which they found themselves, Barbara suggested ways in which they could help themselves to stand back during future encounters and when it was appropriate to do so. They should experiment with these, she said, throughout their time at Redwoods and try to build up their own set of strategies.

It had been a long and intense morning, and Molly headed gratefully for the spa, only to find that several others had had the same idea.

'You know what,' said Tom as the two lounged sumptuously in the outdoor Jacuzzi, 'I could do with a drink, and there's not a chance of getting one round here. Fancy a trip 'downtown'?'

Two hours later, joined by Celia, who had been roped in at dinner, (not entirely under duress), they met at reception and headed downhill towards the bus stop. Arriving downtown they spotted what looked like a cocktail bar sporting a much-welcome happy hour sign and headed hopefully inside.

Two five dollar Long Island Ice Teas and a Moscow Mule later they had forgotten their burden of self-discovery and chatted excitedly about the prospect of a debauched evening ahead.

'Sea lion selfies' yelled Tom in a slurred half shout - which summoned curious glances from the surrounding tables!

'Yeeeess,' screamed Celia in agreement 'Let's head down to the wharf and then hit the boardwalk.'

Amidst giggles from the girls and several overloaded and imposing guffaws from a very merry Tom they set off with gleeful abandon.

Having secured the best arm's length safe distance shots they possibly could and scared some of the bewildered creatures straight off into the sea, they headed for their next stop. Before she knew it, Molly found herself squeezed tightly into a car about to set itself off round the Ghost Train trail.

'But I hate Ghost Trains, I'm too sc…..' she started blurting out as the car revved into action and they rattled off into the darkness, emerging 10 minutes later in a state of gurgling hilarity. 'I didn't know they were allowed to actually touch you!' screeched Celia as she rubbed her arms down disgustedly. The three collapsed into giggles and stumbled out of the car and into the nearest beach bar.

Appearing again in the early hours with a communal sense of homing instinct, they summoned a mini cab and, tumbling out at the front of Redwoods reception in a frenzy of drunken banter, they were greeted at the door by a less than exhilarated Ged.

'It's late,' he barked at them grumpily, standing straight and serious in his fisherman's trousers and clutching a mug of something which wafted lemongrass. 'I suggest you proceed quietly to your rooms and get some rest so that you may not disturb tomorrow's ongoing work, for yourselves or others.'

Supressing their giggles, or in Tom's case guffaws, they bid a hasty farewell to their partners in crime and headed for much - welcome beds.

Chapter 10: Sharing Energy and Enlightenment

In order to clear the cobwebs of the mind and prepare herself for a full morning of study, Molly headed straight to the pool for an early morning swim. As she glided smoothly from one side to the other, occasionally raising her head to feel the morning sunshine rising gradually over the mountain, Molly thought about the next phase of her studies and about whether healing could play an actual part in her everyday life. Or would these few weeks remain as a dream-like vacation from reality? An exploration into the unknown and unaccepted?

Refreshed and ready for breakfast, she headed into the conservatory, only to be joined by a perturbed looking Carola. Shifting her gaze nervously downwards, the colourful American radiated anxiety and restlessness.

'Are you ok?' asked Molly, somewhat reticently, unsure if she wanted to be sucked, right now, into someone else's world of inner dilemmas.

'Just thinking about this crystal I got from my ex, who was pretty aggressive actually. Don't really know what to do with it now. How do you dispose of an object so high in negative energy, and what will be the consequences? As I learn more about the power of crystals I'm starting to regard it differently.'

And more fearfully, thought Molly sceptically. Could objects really expel energy effectively and alter our experiences? She doubted it. Wondering whether what Carola really needed was to let go of her attachments to her 'ex' and move on, she remembered something she had heard once about crystals.

'Can't you cleanse it?'

'But I don't want it anymore' replied Carola, starting to appear more and more agitated.

'How about throwing it into the sea?' asked Molly 'We could go and do it later? Surely the sea is a natural type of, err, energy source?'

Molly felt the anxiety lift as the frazzled woman sitting opposite her considered this idea. She seemed happy with this, and as Molly wondered just what kind of mini disposal ceremony she had let herself in for, she bid a temporary farewell to a happier looking Carola and headed for her classroom.

The first hour was spent talking about 'auras' and 'chakras' – neither of which words Molly warmed to and towards which Tom seemed to be experiencing a similar lack of conviction. Obviously suffering from the over indulgences of the previous night, his facial expression was a mirror of her own internal doubt. As Barbara talked about visualising energy in the most mundane of everyday experiences, whilst watering plants, walking in nature, talking to pets, etc. Tom whispered to his counterpart in scepticism, 'I am about to expel a large amount of energy from my arse...' and exited the room just as they were getting into pairs to try some initial energy healing techniques. Concealing a conspiratorial titter, Molly smiled her way through a preparatory visualisation session and then looked across at her partner, Celia, who, with dark circles under her eyes and a tired sheen across her skin, did not look as though she radiated positive energy in any way today.

'I'll do the healing,' Celia helpfully muttered, and Molly sat with eyes closed while Celia moved her hands in the way they had been instructed.

Nothing. No tingling, no warmth, no feeling of connectivity. Maybe this is what comes of hitting the cocktails on a school night, she thought wearily to herself as she longed, in her gurgling belly, for lunchtime.

As they all emerged from the room and headed for the conservatory, Molly gazed across at Tom, looking marginally less jaded than he had earlier. Catching up with him, she observed that his earlier hangover bravado had been replaced with a look of tired vulnerability, and remembered his quiet and retiring demeanour after Monday's experience - sharing session. He had simply withdrawn to his room quietly for an hour or so before appearing revived and rearing to go in the Jacuzzi after lunch.

'You ok?' she ventured tentatively

'Yeah, head ache gone actually. Just heading to my room for a nap to try and shake this hangover.'

And he was gone. Again tempted to suspend her disbelief, Molly wondered if maybe there wasn't something in this energy sharing lark after all…..

Chapter 11: Journies Into The past

The 'crystal disposal' trip had gone well. They had managed to inject some humour into the process and had wandered along the wharf chatting seamlessly, stopping for a coffee and eventually arriving back at Redwoods at about 6pm, just in time for dinner. Molly had found herself warming to Carola and starting to understand where some of her insecurities lay. She was a 'bad man' magnet (hadn't we all been at some point in our lives?) and a constant stream of such fellows had led to a serious problem with her self-esteem.

As the days went on, Molly and Carola started spending more and more time in each other's company. Molly found herself falling into a steady routine of early morning yoga and meditation, afternoon swim and spa, eating well and beginning to form some potentially lasting friendships. During yet another sunny afternoon lounging round the kidney-shaped pool, the two women found themselves discussing their respective episodes of depression and anxiety.

'I think it's always there with me,' said Carola wistfully, 'I never feel truly happy, only for small glimpses of time.'

'For me it's cyclical,' confessed Molly, ' I go through phases when I have become so high in spirits that it seems the only way to go is down and so, invariably, I spiral out of control. Bipolar episodes of a kind, but, luckily for me, not very often.'

'How about you try your healing on me?' Carola perked up with the idea of this. 'It can't hurt, and you need to practice! I don't mind being a guinea-pig!'

'Let me talk to Barbara…'

Wondering about what she was letting herself in for she slipped into the cooling waters and ruminated over the wisdom of using Carola as her 'human guinea-pig' as she glided around the curves of the pool.

****

That morning's group session was all about trying out the new healing techniques on each other in a safe environment. With one student remaining seated and the other quietly placing hands in the spaces around them, framing their expectant forms with all the energy they could muster, there was a peaceful tranquillity that filled the room and cradled them all with a sense of overwhelming wellbeing. Molly took the opportunity, while still in the grip of this energizing positivity, to approach Barbara and ask her about starting some healing sessions with Carola.

'I don't see why not, as long as you consult me on each stage and make sure she has some sort of support system in place. I believe there's an onsite counsellor should she need to talk.'

Feeling slightly apprehensive about the whole idea Molly thanked Barbara and turned on her heel, only to come smack bang into contact with Tom. The self-assured air seemed to have slipped away and he appeared to be a bundle of nerves.

'Fancy a trip downtown this afternoon?' asked Molly, wondering whether a distraction would help lift his mood.

Affirming in a somewhat reluctant fashion, Tom agreed to meet Molly at 2pm in reception and take a walk down to the waterside.

Two hours later and the sun scorched down on them as they made their way down the mountainside and towards the quay. Sitting by the side of the wharf, the now familiar sight of the barking sea lions felt somewhat comforting. Molly watched as Tom's shoulders lowered slightly in partial relaxation and waited for her new-found friend to come at least part of the way to saying what was on his mind.

'Guess I'm finding all this quite difficult'. He tugged at the plastic catch on his backpack, pulling it backwards and forwards until Molly thought it might give way completely and release the contents of his bag into the waters below.

'Would this be easier over a beer?' Molly ventured.

Rewarded with a small half-hearted grin and a questioning shrug, she tugged him to his feet and the two headed to an open air quay side café.

'I'm starting to realise I might be one of those terrible characters who takes on the role of healer when in fact they actually need healing themselves before they can do any good to anyone.'

'Aren't we all that person just a little bit?' responded Molly, wondering at her own motivations for getting into this altruistic therapy voyage.

'It's cringe-worthy to think, though, that I actually might be of any help to anyone when I am such a gigantic f*** up myself.' Tom let out a strangled chuckle which immediately turned into a more painful sounding sob-like choke.

'The truth is, the deeper I look inside myself the more I'm reminded and the less stable I feel. I normally just bundle on forwards in an illusion of carefree happiness, but at the moment I just don't feel able, it's churning up things I've stored away, and for good reason.'

Tom put his head in his hands and Molly put a tenuous hand on his shoulder, nodding in reassurance and waiting, not wanting to interrupt whatever it was that was coming next.

'It was 25 years ago now,' Tom continued in quiet wobbling tones so that Molly had to lean forward to catch what he was saying.

'He split us apart, he ruined our relationship, and why me? Why not Jake? And is that why I'm like I am now? Was he drawn to me because of who I am? God - was I even being punished?'

Tom's eyes brimmed with tears while Molly patiently rubbed his back, remaining silent while the whole story falteringly unfolded until Tom appeared spent, bent over his half full beer mug like it was a pool that would miraculously reveal a solution for his pain.

25 years ago Tom and his twin brother Jake, at the tender age of nine years old, had been members of a karate club in their local village hall. Both had thrived in this friendly community environment and had started to make quick progress. Tom in particular had excelled at the sport, a fact which secretly thrilled him, since Jake was usually the sporty, brainy, successful twin in his eyes. His competitive streak surfaced and he started staying later for extra tuition, lapping up all the advice he could get from the tutor he idolized.

What a cliché that the tutor who had inspired such confidence should start taking little advantages which soon escalated into something

Tom knew was wrong and yet felt he had somehow invited. When it reached a head one evening, having pushed Tom further than his eagerness to please could accommodate, he left the club, much to everyone's confusion, and withdrew from sports completely, happy to let his brother succeed in his place and taking on instead the role of sharp witted funny man, always ready with a sarcastic retort.

Tom was battling, and had been ever since, with the fear that he had attracted attention from this man because he was different. He had begun to realise, even at such a young age, that he was different from his brother, but it wasn't until the teenage years crept upon them that he realised he might be gay. Still struggling to come to terms with this, he had never spoken openly to his brother or the rest of his family about his sexuality and instead kept it all hidden inside like a huge guilty secret.

Feeling quite drained herself at the enormity of this revelation and at the sight of the crumpled and broken man before her, Molly squeezed Tom as hard as she could muster, downed the rest of her pint and urged Tom to do the same.

'Ready for another?' she asked hopefully with a sheepish grin and an appeal to the humour she knew Tom lived by.

Draining his own glass Tom forced a semi-smile and gazed up at her with an expression that indicated massive relief. 'Why not?'

Chapter 12: Bringing It All Back Home

As the days passed by Molly found herself slotting into routines and relationships with an ease that made her happy she had started on this journey in this wonderful place. She remained unsteady in her convictions about healing but was opening herself up to the experiences that came upon her and to those she shared them with.

One afternoon herself and Carola were lounging in the communal area, with its sunny outlook and inviting floor cushions when they spotted a guitar shoved unceremoniously in a cobwebby corner.

'Oh look!' exclaimed Carola excitedly, 'didn't you say you play?'

A shaft of sunlight cast its spell across the room and placed the instrument in a spotlight which seemed to entice and beckon.

Getting a real sense of 'two worlds collide' Molly hesitated as she contemplated the side of herself she had temporarily pushed aside in her day to day life in this Californian paradise. She made her way tentatively to the other side of the room and inspected the instrument, which had seen better days but had its full complement of strings, and, as a few twangs proved, a decent tone to boot. Tuning up, and wondering what Carola was expecting from her next, she didn't have long to wait.

'What can you play? Can we have a singalong?'

Luckily Molly had had to memorize a range of songs in the course of her job and had taught herself to improvise a set of chord progressions which quite often served her rightly when trying to work out a new song.

She started with a Beatles number, Yesterday, which she reckoned most people knew a few words to. Sure enough Carola crooned along quite happily. And then the requests rushed in, as did other guests, peering inquisitively round the door to see where the music was coming from and getting easily sucked in as they witnessed Carola's overt enthusiasm.

45 minutes and over a dozen songs later, Molly laid down the guitar amidst pleas for more and made her way into the canteen area to get a much needed cuppa. She needed a minute to absent herself from the flurry of attention and digest the familiar feelings of surging joy and satisfaction she was experiencing.

While opening herself to all these new experiences, music had absented itself for a while, and she was just beginning to realise how much she had missed it. How could she forget the overwhelmingly happy feelings her job and her minor role as a musical entertainer gave her on a daily basis? She wondered what on earth she was searching for when music provided such an awesomely grounding basis for a happy existence.

She was soon joined by chattering others, asking her when she would play again and exclaiming at how much they had enjoyed a singsong.

As she sat with her tea and a handful of admirers Carola approached, beaming and content.

'You know,' she started in a persuasive and questioning tone,

'We could substitute some of those healing sessions we've been doing for a good old sing song? I feel like I've just had a week's worth of therapy just from opening my mouth and squawking for all I'm worth!'

It was remarkable how, as calming and meditative as they had proved to be, Molly and Carola's 'hands on' healing sessions had not even scraped the surface of the sort of happiness invoked by half an hour of shared music making. Lifting voices in unison and filling the air with a symphony of sound.

As Molly nodded her smiling consent she was reminded yet again of the therapeutic value of

music and how it never failed to lift her spirits
and return her to a sense of truly satisfied self.

Chapter 13: Sea Life

As their time drew to a close at Redwoods, Molly and her new found friends started to make plans for their next steps outside the retreat. During their last morning session, Barbara asked the group if they had achieved their aims in joining the class and how they imagined themselves moving forwards with what they had learnt.

As each student made their final contribution Molly's mind raced over the events of the last four weeks. She had searched inside herself and found comfort in the fact that others experienced the empathetic tendencies that had previously left her with an overwhelming sense of unease. Exploring these tendencies and how to manage and use them in a productive way had opened her eyes and laid out a pathway of possibilities down which she could travel on her return to London. Most importantly, however, she had come to the realisation that music meant something priceless to her as a healing mechanism and was definitely the channel through which she intended to work in the future. She had made up her mind, however, that on her return to London she would definitely find a healing centre and explore the discipline further.

The effects of the relaxing, peaceful nature of life at Redwoods was evident in everyone around her. Tom now radiated a sort of relieved sense of calm, having been through a personal journey which was long overdue. Carola had developed a new found love of singing, and Celia was practically chomping on a bit of enthusiastic ideas to take back to Los Angeles.

Sitting in the conservatory after yet another wholefood feast, the four discussed how they should celebrate their final days.

'I've always wanted to go dolphin and whale watching,' confessed Molly excitedly. 'I suppose here is one of the best places to do it?'

'And what about a beach party?' added Tom with characteristic verve. 'We could explore one of the beaches we haven't seen before?'

After much animated to-ing and fro-ing of ideas it was decided that they would take a morning boat trip from the wharf, on a medium sized boat, just in case! Then take a couple of hours to clean up and have lunch, and in the afternoon, take the coastal walk to Mitchell's Cove Beach in time to catch the sunset.

The courses having finished on the Friday afternoon, all that remained was the weekend, before everyone would be leaving on Sunday afternoon and heading off in their different directions. Tom and Molly had decided to travel together for a while. Molly was flying out of Los

Angeles in a couple of weeks' time and so they were working on their itinerary. They would be hiring a car, and taking Carola as far as San Francisco.

On Saturday morning, bright and early, the four headed to the wharf for their boat trip. The weather was sunny and breezy (as usual), and, slathered in factor 50, they boarded the craft with their waterproofs and took waterside seats.

30 minutes later, as the sea chopped and bobbed beneath them, eyes peeled and chatter to a minimum, they spotted their first little dolphin, leaping and turning beside the boat. To the left, to the right. They seemed to be on all sides, and the passengers cooed and gasped as they watched the deep sea acrobatics going on all around them. Sprayed by the waves, they all turned as the skipper pointed to a larger commotion in the water where a humpback was rising and falling with the motion of the tides. He jumped and twisted, passengers transfixed.

Eventually the boat headed slowly back to shore, its passengers satiated with contentment.

'It was definitely worth the frizzy hair effect and soggy bottoms,' Carola announced as they trekked back along the harbour front.

'How about the harbour café?' suggested Celia. 'I'm a bit peckish now I've regained my land legs and we could spruce up in the rest room and chill out for a while?

They all agreed this was a good idea, and emerged three hours later with full bellies, partially restored coiffures and a couple of cocktails merrier.

Sunset wasn't until 8.30pm, and so it was decided (primarily by Tom) that the next stop should be a mini mart which sold enough alcohol to keep them happy on the beach.

Armed with wine coolers, cans of cold beer and a couple of bottles of the finest prosecco they could find, they divided their load and headed off along the coastal path to Mitchell's Cove.

Having reached their destination and sat themselves down with a sigh and a groan here and there, they gazed at the view of Monterey Bay, tipple in hand and eyes on the skyline.

'I'm definitely coming back here at some point in the future,' stated Molly decisively.

'It's not far for me,' drawled Carola, 'San Francisco's only up the coast and I think Redwoods does weekend courses too.

As Celia nodded in agreement Tom remained quiet and pensive. His experience had been a more painful one and the association with this may not hasten his return…

Gazing at the skyline as the vastness above them transformed into shades of orangey pink,

Moly gasped and pointed. 'Look! Look at the waves straight ahead!!'

Sure enough, you could just make out the silhouettes of three pirouetting sea mammals, colliding gracefully with the rising waves as though putting on an evening cabaret for the beach goers.

Evening complete and bottles drained, they wobbled their way towards the coastal path and eventually tiptoed through Redwoods reception.

'Have you ever noticed how we're the only ones craving alcohol in this place?' came Celia's slurred and curious whisper.

'Maybe that's what draws the four of us together?' replied Molly questioningly

'Unable to shake off our city issues and suspend our sense of disbelief enough to let that little dependency go!'

Tom's retort was met with a selection of snorts and snuffles as the four headed off to their cosy cabins with a new idea to pervade their dreams.

As usual, Molly drifted off the moment her head hit the pillow, transported once again to a coastal location where she hovered by the water as the waves rippled. Dipping her hand in, she saw a creature approaching and glanced backward to where her friends had stood. As they disappeared in to the background she was torn as to whether to leap up and follow their retreat or remain by the water side and trust in the oncoming shape which loomed ahead of her. Closing her eyes, she felt smooth skin brush her palm and looked downwards to see a small grey dolphin gliding past her.

She awoke with a feeling of overwhelming calm, knowing that she should trust in whatever lay ahead of her and not look back. Today she would begin the second stage of her Californian adventure.

Chapter 14: Making Tracks

Sunday morning arrived with a cloudy humidity, and, after a sociable breakfast time mingling of friends saying their heartfelt farewells, Carola, Molly and Tom gathered in reception, waiting for the delivery of the hire car they would be driving to San Francisco and beyond. Celia had already set off for Los Angeles, where they would visit her in seven days or so.

Car delivered efficiently and final goodbyes all done, they set out along Highway 1 on the two hour drive to Carola's hometown. Their route would take them past Pescadiro, Half Moon Bay and Pacifica, with stretches of gorgeous wild coastline creating opportunities for spectacular viewing along the way. Molly, attracted to the romanticism of the name, had already pinpointed Half Moon Bay as a little stop along the way. They searched for a suitable lunch spot, making their way down little streets filled with antique stalls, art galleries and curiosity shops, Molly finding a little jewellery stall from which she purchased a silver half - moon necklace. A trinket to remind her of her travels on inevitable gloomy winter days back in the UK.

Carola had offered to put the pair up on her sofa bed for the couple of nights they planned to be in San Francisco, and as they parked up around the back of her apartment block in the LGBTQ district of the city, Molly felt a sense of excitement at what lay ahead of her.

After settling in and freshening up, the three headed out to dinner at a local Thai restaurant not far from Carola's apartment. The restaurant had a delightful little garden filled with charming stone water features and a splattering of smiling Buddha statues. The temperature was perfect and after a lovely meal of delicious fragrant dishes, the three sat back in contentment to enjoy a second bottle of Sauvignon Blanc.

'I think I'll try going it alone for a while,' stated Carola wistfully,

'Over the last few weeks I've come to realize that my choice of men has never been the best and that I've actually been terrified of being on my own. It's time to find out a little bit more about myself. Who knows, I might even join a singing group!'

Smiling encouragingly and discussing her options and choices, the three managed to while away the next couple of hours with, as usual, a drink in hand and an eye on their individual futures.

They finally left, Tom sloping shyly off to explore the night life, and the two women heading back to Carola's place to enjoy a hot drink and a night time chat, before Molly, struggling to keep her eyes open after a long day's drive in the sunshine, drifted off to sleep with screen shots of Californian adventures playing through her mind.

The next few days saw sunny mornings and moments of chilly afternoon fog.

While Carola resumed her day to day life in 'Revelations', Tom and Molly explored the city for all they were worth. A walk to Haight Ashbury with its 60s psychedelic vibes, a longed-for ride on a cable car, where the driver allowed Molly to take hold of the controls for a minute or more (much to her horror and delight), a two-mile hike across Golden Gate Bridge, where fog floated across the cables and surrounded them so that they felt like they were wandering into a lost and enticing land, and a day trip to Berkley, the home of ideas, which reflected the hustle and bustle of student life.

All too soon it was time to say goodbye to Carola and head off on the next leg of their Californian journey. With Tom at the wheel, they traced their way back along the coast line towards Los Angeles, music blaring from the stereo and singing voices raised in appreciation.

Road Trip Day 1:

First stop Carmel by the Sea. A couple of hours drive down the coast and a pleasant afternoon spent browsing little art galleries ('over 100 in all', as Molly quoted from the guide book) and spotting dogs galore! They had never seen so many well-pampered pooches in one place, trotting along tree-lined avenues in the most charming of neighbourhoods. Again, seduced by a name, the two headed east of Highway 1 into the Carmel Valley, to 'Folklore' winery, hidden amongst the vineyards and boasting a beautiful courtyard dining area where the two whiled away a few hours, accompanied by a six wine tasting menu and feast of various cheeses complimented by succulent heirloom tomatoes.

Emboldened by wine, Tom relayed stories of his life as a twin and confessed to how he had let the closeness between himself and his brother drift since he had moved to California.

'He (Jake) has no notion of the angst I've been through over the past few years,' Tom wistfully told Molly, herself resisting the wine since she had promised to take on the drive back to Monterey.

'How can I even come out to him, let alone expect him to believe what happened when we were children?'

'Why do you think he wouldn't understand?' asked Molly. 'Don't you think he may have suspected something wasn't right?'

The laugh that preceded Tom's answer had a bitter edge as he tried to paint a picture to Molly of the brother he knew.

'Jake is everybody's best friend and probably the most easy going fella you'll ever meet. I'm not saying he buries his head in the sand, but I just can't imagine talking to him about anything of any emotional gravity. Our closeness was unspoken, as was the fierce sense of loyalty in our relationship. Also, I don't know when I'll see him again, it's not the kind of conversation you have over the phone.

'Hey, thinking about it, you should meet up with him when you get back to London. He's great company and has a real love of music. Yes! I'm 'gonna hook you up!'

Tom, whose spirits suddenly seemed to have been lifted at the idea of matchmaking across oceans, garbled on excitedly on the subject of Jake's attributes, fuelled by wine and the power of positive memories.

They finally left at sunset and headed back along the coastline to Monterey, where they had booked into a reasonably priced hostel for the night, lured by the promise of a 'make your own pancakes' breakfast.

Road Trip Day 2:
The breakfast having lived up to its promises, and consequently feeling slightly sick and over sugared, Tom and Molly started out on Day two of their road trip. For Molly, this promised to be the highlight of the trip, fulfilling her fantasy

of traversing The Big Sur, evocative to her of the many TV shows and songs that were famous by association.

'The Lonely Planet describes it as a 'state of mind,' she quoted at Tom as they headed out along the 90 miles of craggy coastline that spanned the Pacific Ocean. Approaching Bixby Bridge, Molly searched for the Michael Kiwanuka song that had been used as 'Big Little Lies' soundtrack, the series being one of the reasons she had been so keen to see 'The Big Sur' for herself.

'Did you ever wan' it? Did you wan' it bad?......' she crooned in the ear of a cringing and slightly hung over Tom, who, despite himself, was taken aback at the magnificence of the structure and its surrounding views. Crumbling cliffs meeting coastline landscapes.

Half an hour later, standing on the breath taking Pfeiffer beach, with its quartz and garnet laced purple sand, The Big Sur seemed to be living up to its reputation. A lunch stop, and then an hour or so drive to Limekiln State Park, where the two planned to camp for the night. Again, they found themselves amongst the redwoods, in a yurt village with decking, hot tubs, and an orchestra of throaty frogs.

Tom hit the sack early. Several heavy nights out in San Francisco, topped by the previous night's indulgences, had finally taken their toll.

Consequently, Molly found herself alone on the creaking deck, night lights twinkling around her, serenaded by the songs of croaking frogs. Being on the road was, she realized, as freeing and joyful as she had always imagined. Gone were the responsibilities and worries of day to day life. The drudgery of routine simply didn't exist as you trundled happily from one sunshiny destination to another, with only the whereabouts of your next meal to worry about. Her sense of self was no longer hampered by workplace or family politics, and while money lasted she could drift between places where nobody knew her, forging a temporary sense of identity unfettered by expectation. Sighing with contentment, she headed for bed with a sense of excited anticipation for tomorrow, satisfied with the idea that only the physical journey itself lay ahead of her.

With one more day's drive to Los Angeles, Molly and Tom planned a final stop along the way. A Beach Inn near Morro Rock, where they hoped to spot peregrine falcons and sea otters. Then a three- hour drive to LA, where the two would part company once and for all, and Molly would head back to the UK, leaving Tom to his life in San Jose. Having parked in the carpark, the two followed the trail down to the beach to see the rock itself. Armed with sea shoes for clambering over stones and ready for another beautiful sunset, they headed out along the rocky beach, dodging the throngs of seagulls as they went.

'What's that?' asked Tom in excitedly hushed tones. Molly followed his gaze to see a small furry creature twisting and turning in the water. Then another, and another until the water seemed teeming with somersaulting bundles.

Perching on a nearby spacious ledge, they waited patiently for the skies to turn orange, scanning the cliffs, now, for the sight of falcon-sized birds.

'Look!' exclaimed Molly, as an unusually large bird not, for once, resembling a seagull swooped over the rock and disappeared somewhere along the cliff face. Happy with idea that they had spotted a falcon, even be it of spurious identity, the day seemed complete.

As it was starting to get late, the two headed back to the car, happy with their quota of wildlife spotting, and walking briskly under chocolate box skies in order to avoid getting totally submerged in the oncoming darkness.

When they arrived at Beach Inn they freshened and then headed out to the communal area for a barbeque. Molly was delighted to see fire pits and noticed that people were already gathering around them. Taking a plate of food, they huddled round one of the pits, grabbing available deckchairs, and soon found themselves in conversation with other holiday makers. Laughing as they recounted tales of Redwood antics and trying their best to explain the healing mission they had been on, the other guests smiled awkwardly.

As others drifted off to their cabins Molly and Tom found themselves still staring into the embers.

'I suppose we sound like two new age hippies seeking to bring our magical powers to the masses', Molly commented with a hint of the old cynicism.

'It's hard to explain Redwoods to outsiders,' mused Tom, 'My experience is definitely one to keep to myself, but I'm glad to have some friends who can relate to what it's all about.' Then, after a thoughtful pause: 'We will keep in touch won't we? I don't want to forget the benefits of this experience and go back to where I left off?'

'It's a kind of transformation which none of us will forget in a hurry, and of course we'll keep in touch. Skype and email are a mere tap away from reality.'

Tom sighed and rose creakily from the deckchair, casting one last glance at the fading embers. 'Come on then, we've got another three-hour drive tomorrow, so let's hit the sack.'

Road Trip Day 3:

They rose early in a quest to find the City of Angels and re-unite with the friend they had left behind just over a week ago. Molly had just three days left before flying out of Los Angeles City Airport, and she wanted to make the most of the rest of her time in sunny California.

Celia lived in a light and airy two-bed apartment in the hipster district of Silver Lake. Having spent the last few days mainly eating and driving, Molly was pleased to learn that Celia had planned some healthy activities for their stay.

First stop Silver Lake Reservoir and a two and a quarter mile loop jog round before dinner. Having spent the last few days sitting, sleeping and eating, Molly and Tom felt glad to get moving, and felt considerably better (if slightly sweaty and out of breath) after, in their case, a steady run, in Celia's, a healthy sprint!

After eating at a tiny local Italian place, Celia had planned a trip to see some live music. Known for its Indie rock, they headed to one of the area's local music bars and spent the remainder of the evening wallowing in the dark sombre sounds of 'Timbre Evening Echo'. Many 'Dark and Stormys' sunk and much news caught up on.

Day 4 – Welcome to Los Angeles

Celia had to work in the studio the following day – but while Tom lounged with CNN, Molly accompanied her to the first yoga class of the day, a 7.30am 'Rocket' Vinyasa flow. As she swept in and out of downward dog Molly wondered about her oncoming return to reality. Would she simply slide back into her daily routine or had she turned a corner and opened herself up to a whole new world of experiences?

Feeling focused and ready for the day, Molly headed back to the apartment in Silver Lake, where Tom was waiting to head out to the Hollywood Hills and spot the all famous sign, a photo opportunity not to be missed. The two hiked round Griffith Park, getting all the best shots before heading back to cook dinner for their host.

Lounging around a prettily lit balcony table, bellies full of rich alcoholic beverages and mushroom risotto and lips stained with wine, the three vowed to maximise on their experiences and track each other's progress.

'Would I be right in saying we all discovered extra little bits of ourselves at Redwoods and forged some sort of plan for a path forwards?' asked Celia, who remained excited about expanding her studio timetable to include more meditative classes which embraced some sort of healing philosophy. She admitted she was not currently sure how this would go. She would have to search for suitable instructors who would adopt an accessible approach.

'I think we all still have a certain amount of hidden cynicism,' began Molly. (Wry smiles from Tom and a tentative nod from Celia.) 'But, if nothing else, I have consolidated my love for music and refreshed my enthusiasm for my work. I know I am on the right path, just one that needs enhancing a little.'

Tom remained silent, but there was an unspoken acknowledgement from the three of them that his experience had been the most transformative, and that for him life would never be the same again.

Day 5: Seaside Predictions

Often referred to as 'free- spirited' and with a boardwalk teeming with artists, performers and unorthodox vendors from all walks of life, Venice Beach charmed Tom and Molly with its eccentric hustle and bustle. Having taken in the eye- opening sights of Muscle Beach and explored a plethora of out- of-the- way alleys, they found themselves in the eye line of a sparkly-eyed lady armed with tarot and runes, and dared each other to take the plunge.

'I will if you will......?' Tom's immortal words as he handed over his $10 and plonked himself down behind an elasticated satin curtain to discover his fate.

'I will never tell!' he proclaimed 15 minutes later as he emerged with a wink and gestured for Molly to take her turn.

A frown crossed the face of the lady with the cards and Molly shifted uneasily in her seat.

'You are abandoning aspects of yourself.' She stated mysteriously. 'Don't you ever indulge your feminine self? You are in danger of succumbing to the famous saying: 'All work and no play'. Think of the wiles of your sex and open yourself to encounters!'

Molly blushed and half suppressed an indignant 'tut'. Weren't her mum and her sister always hinting at the man-shaped space in her life? Wasn't she always ignoring their attempts, continuing her life without succumbing to the 'wiles of her sex.' And wasn't she perfectly content?

She smiled sweetly as she handed over her dollars and brushed the comments out of her mind. Tom angled for her to reveal her secrets in vain while she pushed aside the niggle that was starting to rear its persistent head. Expectations. As her journey ended that's where she would find herself. Her mum's expectations of what her life would be, Eva's expectations of what her trip had been, her bosses expectations of what she should achieve, and, most daunting of all, she now realised, her own expectations of herself.

These, she realised, were a mountain to climb with which she simply could not contend. The only person in her life who made no demands on her was, as far as she could see, her father, with his accepting nature and quiet belief in her abilities. As she thought of her father's unerring and unconditional love for her a Tori Amos song lyric came to mind: 'He says - when you 'gonna make up your mind? When you 'gonna love you as much as I do?' When indeed. Self - love was easy when you were on the move without a care in the world, but in a demanding reality of day to day life, finding a self that Molly actually liked and believed in was something she would have to work on.

Chapter 15: Homecoming

The day of Molly's return flight to the UK came in an instant, and before she knew it she was standing in a queue for security while Tom and Celia waved frantically from actual LA. Blowing her last kiss, she disappeared through the archway as a stern looking officer frisked her with a scary looking implement.

Leaning forwards in her slightly cramped economy seat she searched through the inflight films, determined to escape to another world while she sat captive in this metallic capsule no-man's land. When the lights went out, she slipped on her headphones, and wistfully absorbed herself in the jangling tones of 'Timbre Evening Echo' and their reminder of LA evenings.

After 10 plus hours in the skies Molly felt a familiar relief to be strolling past W H Smith's and Costa and heading out into a late summer morning with bright skies and more than a British quota of sunshine. True to her word, there stood Eva by the National Express coach stop, ready to transport her back to the studio to which she hadn't given a second thought throughout her four weeks away.

'Now I know why you nagged me so hard for so long about travelling', she told Eva as they clambered into the rubbish strewn mini.

'I feel utterly refreshed and yet totally spent. Filled with ideas of new found freedom and ready to go again right now if I had the chance!'

Eva squealed with excitement and begged for details as the two weaved their way through the London traffic and finally drew to a halt in the familiar Islington Housing Estate. Molly sighed as she turned her key in the lock, both glad to be home after her 12+hour journey and disappointed to have ended such an exciting chapter of her story.

As usual, Molly drifted off about two minutes after her head hit her London pillow that night. She sank into a much needed sleep, filled with screen shots of Californian adventures and hazy mixed up glimpses of what may lie ahead.

Chapter 16: New Beginnings

After two weeks falling back into familiar routines Molly found herself facing life in London with a new found curiosity. Glad to be back at work, she faced the challenge of working with two troubled adult clients with mental health difficulties - moving away temporarily from the familiarity of working with children.

While one of the two sought to overcome the shyness brought on by her struggle to come to terms with her learning difficulty, the second had been grappling for years with a crippling depression that overwhelmed her ability to live a contented day to day life. Molly met these challenges with a new sense of enthusiasm and a new found energy for research into new methods and techniques for therapy.

Aside from all of this, she was attempting to squirrel away some of this energy for her own use before it was all zapped.

She had got into contact with the London Healing Centre to find out more about becoming a voluntary part time practitioner, and had also unexpectedly received an email from one of her musical acquaintances, suggesting a collaboration for an oncoming open mic.

She was attempting to keep hold of that sense of unfettered self she had found in California and apply it now in the forging of a new kind of confidence. Working with adults was helping her to understand the complex web of insecurities that could stand in the way as one trod the rocky pathway to self - acceptance. She had developed, however, a new sense of enthusiasm for making music and a longing to share this whenever possible. Her appreciation for her family had also reared a happy head and she was able to actually look forward to family gatherings in a way she had not done since childhood.

****

Sitting around a treat laden table, lapping up the lingering rays of a fading summer, Molly smiled a satisfied smile as her parents leafed through a carefully hand picked selection of California photos.

'It all looks very exotic' trilled Joan, feigning an excited interest while piling plates ready for clearing.

Barry, on the other hand, waited until his devoted wife had disappeared into the kitchen and leaned across the table with a question for his youngest daughter.

'Did you find what you were looking for?' he asked quietly with an inquiring smile.

Molly thought for a moment.

'I think most of it was here already. It was just a matter of seeing things through new eyes.'

Barry leaned back looking slightly disappointed and Molly wondered whether there was really much to be found. The secret to a happy life wasn't hidden at the end of a colourful treasure trail was it?

Chapter 17: A New Friend

Covent Garden buzzed as Molly wove her way through throngs of busy shoppers and away from the peace of Hop Gardens and the Healing Centre where she had just spent the past two hours. The training she was receiving there was opening up even more questions about the nature of hands on healing in her mind. She wasn't convinced she had the gift or certainly the conviction that she could help people through that medium and was beginning to see that her talents may lie elsewhere. Her commitment to music therapy had increased full fold and she was amazed and relieved to find that stepping away from her vocation for a while had proved to be a step forward in forging her chosen career.

Stopping for a moment to scan the Christmas ornamented window of a colourful Paperchase, lured by the idea of novelty stationary and unnecessaries and just about to step over the threshold, Molly's phone rang, and she flipped back the protective case, stepped to the side and trilled her hello.

'Hi. Is this Molly?' A low and slightly familiar sounding voice asked tentatively.

'Yes, it is. Who's this please?' trying to place the tone, curious and yet slightly irritated that her shopping trip had been interrupted.

'Hi. This is Jake, Tom's brother' (sounding slightly embarrassed)

'Oh! Hello!' taken aback, pleased and even more curious.

'Tom suggested I link up with you. He got back in touch and told me so much about you. I figured I should try and make a connection with the lady who brought my brother back to me!'

Flattered, Molly exclaimed at how pleased she was Tom had got back in touch and ranted about how happy she'd been to meet him.

Jake laughed, and after a few more exchanges Molly found herself agreeing to a meet up. A Saturday night in Camden no less. Feeling somewhat irritated with Tom for his obviousness but also interested to meet the brother she had heard so much about, Molly flipped closed her phone and continued about her business with a little more bounce in her step and a sense of something to look forward to.

****

After a busy working week, two steps forward and two back with her clients at work and a few uneventful nights in front of the TV, Saturday came along and Molly found herself outside the

Lock Tavern, shifting from foot to foot in the chilly November air, as a tall, dark, less neatly turned out version of her Californian partner in crime strode confidently towards her.

What struck her most was the sense of calm and laid back self-assured air Tom's brother possessed. All the angst his brother had endured had obviously passed Jake by, and yet he possessed the same wit-laced charm with none of the cynically bitter edge that had made Molly smile on so many occasions.

It was unclear how much Tom had told his brother about his Californian transformation, and Molly found herself biting back her tongue as she discussed her holiday and the experiences Tom and herself had shared.

Jake proved to be exceptionally good company, and the evening passed easily and quickly, with a few too many drinks consumed but definitely enjoyed. They parted company with the agreement that they would re-connect soon, before the Christmas rush, and hugged warmly on the tube platform before Jake disappeared with the closing doors and rattled into the tunnel out of view, and, disappointingly, out of mind for the time being.

Chapter 18: Welcome Additions

The warmth of the Christmas season pervaded Molly's mood – she loved this time of year, and as she cycled to work on a bright frosty morning, California seemed a world away, and yet she was happy to bask in the chill of this wintery London world.

Her mind turned to Josie, the client with depression she had been treating for the past couple of months. Josie's depression was long term, and originated from childhood, a complicated combination of family problems and chemicals off kilter. Josie had responded particularly well to singing, preferring already penned songs to writing, which Molly was hoping to progress to as time went on and Josie's confidence in her own abilities increased.

Molly had toyed with the idea of bringing in Christmas songs (which she herself loved!), but feared the emotive connection to a time of, for many, loneliness and pressure to succumb to the surrounding social whirl would be difficult for Josie to relate to.

Instead she had opted for the classic Bill Withers 'Lovely Day', with its myriad opportunities for improvisation and harmony.

As she set up the room, collection of percussion and drum kit at the ready, the door opened and in walked Josie with a wonderful surprise in toe. The friendliest little bundle of joy, turning out to be a Chihuahua/ Jack Russell cross, bounded in and settled itself at Josie's feet.

Josie explained that she had been meaning to get an emotional support dog for a while. 'Dougie' had become available and had already proved himself invaluable, calming her when panic attacks threatened and staying by her side as she battled her daily life.

Was it Molly's imagination, or did Josie's smile radiate that day as she crooned along with Bill Withers and attempted one after another improvisation with a voice that promised a building confidence?

As soon as the session finished and the room was restored to a quiet, tidy, organised silence, ready for the next client to bring it to life, Molly made her way to the office and begged the manager's ear.

'Therapy dogs!' she exclaimed excitedly. 'How about a centre dog, who attends sessions when needed and exudes a general calm presence, comforting clients and brightening the whole place up?'

It wasn't an immediate no, and after much discussion it was decided that it may be possible. Jenny, the receptionist, had been meaning to get a pet and was willing to take him or her home at night and bring the dog in for daily sessions.

Molly left work that day on a high, inspired by the idea that her own life could be considerably improved by the surrogate pet who would brighten her working life at the centre. She had always loved animals, and now her mind was reeling with ideas of animal therapy and how this could be a new road to follow.

Chapter 19: Celebrations

'I was following the… I was following the…. I was following the….'

It was the evening of the Music Therapy Centre's Christmas benefit, and Molly was standing at the front of a tinsel decked hall conducting a group of clients in their performance of Fleet Foxes' 'White Winter Hymnal'. They were doing well, and Molly's nerves were laced with the urge to fight back the lump which was rising in her throat. Voices were soaring, candles flickered on tables and you could hear a pin drop as the respectful audience drank in the Christmas atmosphere.

As she turned to gesture to her singers and they all bowed with joy and relief, she caught a glimpse of Jake in the audience, giving her an enthusiastic thumbs up and giving off his usual air of calm and charm. The combination could be good for Molly, she recognised, and it was great to have such good company for weekend meet ups and more.

At the same time she had never felt so in charge of her career and submerged in her total love of music. Watching her group proudly as Melody, their new therapy puppy, wound her way excitedly amongst them, Molly wondered what her next step would be and where her life would take her.

California had reinforced her sense of belonging in a city she loved and incidentally encouraged her to fall in love with music all over again. Travel was a bonus, and she was sure more adventures would raise their heads, but a sense of belonging was priceless.

As an electric guitar riff cut through the chat, Molly turned to see Jakob approach the microphone and stomp his feet as his dad accompanied him:

'Get yer rocks off,
Get yer rocks off honey,
Shake 'em now now,
Get 'em off down town'

Smiling at the new found audacity of this eight-year-old and his song choice, the song which had marked a turning point in his progress, Molly joined the audience, sat back and enjoyed the performance - of which she was both part and purveyor. The performance would go on and she would keep up with it for as long as she could, wherever and with whomever she found herself.

Track Listing: The Sounds Of Molly's Journey:

1. Joni Mitchell: 'California'
2. Primal Scream: 'Rocks'
3. Ed Sheeran: 'Shape of You'
4. Tao Cruz: 'Dynamite'
5. Justin Beiber: 'Love Yourself'
6. All About Eve: 'More than the Blues'
7. The Beatles: 'Yesterday'
8. Michael Kiwanuka: 'Cold Little Heart'
9. Tori Amos: 'Winter'
10. Bill Withers: 'Lovely Day'
11. The Fleet Foxes: 'White Winter Hymnal'

Main Sources of Research/Further Reading:

1.   Ewens, Hannah, 2018, '*Super Empaths are Real, Says Study,*' *https://www.vice.com/en/article/xwj84k/super-empaths-are-real-says-study*

2.   Mason, Su, 2010, '*Spiritual Healing: What is it? Does it work and does it have a place in modern health care?*' https://www.rcpsych.ac.uk/docs/default-source/members/sigs/spirituality-spsig/su-mason-spiritual-healing-in-modern-healthcare-x.pdf?sfvrsn=4fc21449

3.   Orloff, Judith, *Judith Orloff M.D.,* (homepage), 2021, drjudithorloff.com/quizzes/are-you-a-physical-empath (*quotes page 31)

4.   Schulte-Peevers, Andrea, *California,* The Lonely Planet, 8th Edition, February 2018

About the Author

Rachael Cook wrote Looking for Melody during the first lockdown in London, UK. She has a degree in English Literature and Sociology and keeps very busy nowadays with her job as an ESOL teacher. When she is not working she enjoys making music with her friends and runs her own small community choir. She has travelled extensively both in California and other worldwide destinations but has settled in the city of London, where she now resides.